ROALD DAHL'S

WONDERFUL MR WILLY WONKA

working in partnership with

National Literacy Trust

ILLUSTRATED BY QUENTIN BLAKE

PUFFIN

PUFFIN BOOKS

UK | USA | Canada | Ireland | Australia
India | New Zealand | South Africa

Puffin Books is part of the Penguin Random House group of companies
whose addresses can be found at global.penguinrandomhouse.com.

www.penguin.co.uk   www.puffin.co.uk   www.ladybird.co.uk

Penguin
Random House
UK

Made for McDonald's 2017
001

Charlie and the Chocolate Factory: first published in the USA by Alfred A Knopf, Inc., 1964;
first published in Great Britain by George Allen & Unwin 1967
Published in paperback by Puffin Books

Printed in Slovakia

A CIP catalogue record for this book is available from the British Library

ISBN: 978–0–141–38637–9

The National Literacy Trust is a registered charity no. 1116260 and a company limited
by guarantee no. 5836486 registered in England and Wales and a registered charity in
Scotland no. SC042944. Registered address: 68 South Lambeth Road, London SW8 1RL.
National Literacy Trust logo and reading tips copyright © National Literacy Trust, 2017
www.literacytrust.org.uk/donate

Batch nr: 128355/51

FSC
MIX
FSC® C022120

Meet
WONDERFUL
MR WILLY WONKA!

He's the most **EXTRAORDINARY**
chocolate maker in the world.
Little **CHARLIE BUCKET**, who lives
in a draughty old house with his
family, is eager to discover what
strange and magical stories surround
the **MYSTERIOUS** owner of the
most **FAMOUS** chocolate
factory ever created.

Turn to the
back of your book
for **STICKERS**
and a handy
BOOKMARK

SEARCH and FIND!
What **COLOUR** is
GRANDPA JOE'S SCARF?

THE FAMOUS CHOCOLATE FACTORY

In the evenings, after he had finished a supper of watery cabbage soup, Charlie Bucket always went into the room of his four grandparents to listen to their stories, and then afterwards to say good night.

Every one of these old people was over ninety. They were as shrivelled as prunes, and as bony as skeletons, and throughout the day, until Charlie made his appearance, they lay huddled in their one bed, two at either end, with nightcaps on to keep their heads warm, dozing the time away with nothing to do. But as soon as they heard the door opening, and heard Charlie's voice saying, 'Good evening, Grandpa Joe and Grandma Josephine, and Grandpa George and Grandma Georgina,' then all four of them would suddenly sit up, and their old wrinkled faces would light up with smiles of pleasure – and the talking would begin. For they loved this little boy. He was the only bright thing in their lives, and his evening visits were something that they looked forward to all day long. Often, Charlie's mother and father would come in as well, and stand by the door, listening to the stories that the old people told; and thus, for perhaps half an hour every night, this room would become a happy place.

One evening, when Charlie went in to see his grandparents, he said to them, 'Is it *really* true that Wonka's chocolate factory is the biggest in the world?'

'*True?*' cried all four of them at once. 'Of course it's true!

Good heavens, didn't you know *that*?
It's about *fifty* times as big as any other!'

'And is Mr Willy Wonka *really* the
cleverest chocolate maker in the world?'

'My *dear* boy,' said Grandpa Joe,

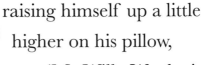

Colour me in!

raising himself up a little
higher on his pillow,

'Mr Willy Wonka is
the most *amazing*,

the most *fantastic*, the most *extraordinary* chocolate maker the world has ever seen! I thought *everybody* knew that!'

'I knew he was famous, Grandpa Joe, and I knew he was very clever . . .'

'*Clever!*' cried the old man. 'He's more than that! He's a *magician* with chocolate! He can make *anything* – anything he wants! Isn't that a fact, my dears?'

The other three old people nodded their heads slowly up and down, and said, '*Absolutely* true. *Just* as true as can be.'

And Grandpa Joe said, 'You mean to say I've never *told* you about Mr Willy Wonka and his factory?'

'Never,' answered little Charlie.

'Good heavens above! I don't know what's the matter with me!'

'Will you tell me now, Grandpa Joe, please?'

'I certainly will. Sit down beside me on the bed, my dear, and listen carefully.'

Grandpa Joe was the oldest of the four grandparents. He was ninety-six and a half, and that is just about as old as anybody can be. Like all extremely old people, he was delicate and weak, and throughout the day he spoke very little. But in the evenings, when Charlie, his beloved grandson, was in the room, he seemed in some marvellous way to grow quite young again. All his tiredness fell away from him, and he became as eager and excited as a young boy.

'Oh, what a man he is, this Mr Willy Wonka!' cried

Grandpa Joe. 'Did you know, for example, that he has himself invented more than two hundred new kinds of chocolate bars, each with a different centre, each far sweeter and creamier and more delicious than anything the other chocolate factories can make!'

'Perfectly true!' cried Grandma Josephine. 'And he sends them to *all* the four corners of the earth! Isn't that so, Grandpa Joe?'

'It is, my dear, it is. And to all the kings and presidents of the world as

well. But it isn't
only chocolate
bars that he

makes. Oh, dear me, no! He has some
really *fantastic* inventions up his sleeve,
Mr Willy Wonka has! Did you know
that he's invented a way of making
chocolate ice cream so that it stays cold
for hours and hours without being in
the refrigerator? You can even leave it
lying in the sun all morning on a hot
day and it won't go runny!'

'But that's *impossible*!' said little

Charlie, staring at his grandfather.

'Of course it's impossible!' cried Grandpa Joe. 'It's completely *absurd*! But Mr Willy Wonka has done it!'

'Quite right!' the others agreed, nodding their heads. 'Mr Wonka has done it.'

'And then again,' Grandpa Joe went on speaking very slowly now so that Charlie wouldn't miss a word, 'Mr Willy Wonka can make marshmallows that taste of violets, and rich caramels that change colour every ten

12

seconds as you suck them, and
little feathery sweets that melt
away deliciously the moment you put
them between your lips. He can make
chewing-gum that never loses its taste,
and sugar balloons that you can blow
up to enormous sizes before you pop
them with a pin and gobble them up.
And, by a most secret method, he can
make lovely blue
birds' eggs with black
spots on them, and when you put one
of these in your mouth, it gradually

gets smaller and smaller until suddenly there is nothing left except a tiny little pink sugary baby bird sitting on the tip of your tongue.'

Grandpa Joe paused and ran the point of his tongue slowly over his lips. 'It makes my mouth water just *thinking* about it,' he said.

Little Charlie sat very still on the edge of the bed, staring at his grandfather. Charlie's face was bright, and his eyes were stretched so wide you could see the whites all around. 'Is all this *really* true?' he asked. 'Or are you pulling my leg?'

'It's true!' cried all four of the old people at once. 'Of course it's true! Ask anyone you like!'

RUMOUR MILL

Charlie isn't sure how to separate fact from fiction when it comes to rumours about Willy Wonka! Can you help him remember what Grandpa Joe told him by circling TRUE or FALSE under these statements?

Wonka's chocolate factory is the biggest in the world.

TRUE or **FALSE**

Wonka invented fifteen
different types of chocolate bar.

TRUE or **FALSE**

Wonka created edible red
birds' eggs with black spots.

TRUE or **FALSE**

Wonka invented chocolate ice
cream that never melts.

TRUE or **FALSE**

Answers on page 62

THE GOOD NEWS

'And I'll tell you something else that's true,' said Grandpa Joe, and now he leaned closer to Charlie, and lowered his voice to a soft, secret whisper. '*Nobody . . . ever . . . comes . . . out!*'

'Out of where?' asked Charlie.

'*And . . . nobody . . . ever . . . goes . . . in!*'

'In *where*?' cried Charlie.

'Wonka's factory, of course! All factories,' said Grandpa Joe, 'have workers streaming in and out of the gates in the mornings and evenings –

except Wonka's! Have *you* ever seen a single person going into that place – or coming out?'

Little Charlie looked slowly around at each of the four old faces, one after the other, and they all looked back at him. They were friendly smiling faces, but they were also quite serious. There was no sign of joking or leg-pulling on any of them.

'Well? Have *you*?' asked Grandpa Joe.

'I . . . I really don't know, Grandpa,' Charlie stammered. 'Whenever I walk past the factory, the gates seem to be closed.'

'You see, Charlie,' he said, 'not so very long ago there used to be thousands of people working in Mr Willy Wonka's factory. Then one day, all of a sudden, Mr Wonka

20

had to ask *every single one of them* to leave, to go home, never to come back.'

'But why?' asked Charlie.

'Because of spies.'

'Spies?'

'Yes. All the other chocolate makers, you see, had begun to grow jealous of the wonderful sweets that Mr Wonka was making, and they started sending in spies to steal his secret recipes. The spies took jobs in the Wonka factory, pretending that they were ordinary workers, and while they were there, each one of them found out exactly how a certain special thing was made.'

'And did they go back to their own factories and tell?' asked Charlie.

'They must have,' answered Grandpa Joe, 'because soon after that, Fickelgruber's factory started making an ice cream that would never melt, even in the hottest sun. Then Mr Prodnose's factory came out with a chewing-gum that never lost its flavour however much you chewed it. And then Mr Slugworth's factory began making sugar balloons that you could blow up to huge sizes before you popped them with a pin and gobbled them up. And so on, and so on. And Mr Willy Wonka tore his beard and shouted, "This is terrible! I shall be ruined! There are spies everywhere! I shall have to close the factory!"'

'But he didn't do that!' Charlie said.

'Oh, yes he did. He told *all* the workers that he was sorry, but they

would have to go home. Then, he
shut the main gates and fastened them
with a chain. And suddenly, Wonka's
giant chocolate factory became silent
and deserted. The chimneys stopped
smoking, the machines stopped
whirring, and from then on, not a single
chocolate or sweet was made. Not a
soul went in or out, and even Mr Willy
Wonka himself disappeared completely.

'Months and months went by,'
Grandpa Joe went on, 'but still
the factory remained closed. And

everybody said, "Poor Mr Wonka. He was so nice. And he made such marvellous things. But he's finished now. It's all over."

'Then something astonishing happened. One day, early in the morning, thin columns of white smoke were seen to be coming out of the tops of the tall chimneys of the factory! People in the town stopped and stared.

"What's going on?" they cried.
"Someone's lit the furnaces! Mr Wonka
must be opening up again!" They ran
to the gates, expecting to see them wide
open and Mr Wonka standing there to
welcome his workers back.

'But no! The great iron gates were still
locked and chained as securely as ever,
and Mr Wonka was nowhere to be seen.
But there was no question at all that
the factory was running. And it's gone
on running ever since, for these last
ten years. What's more, the chocolates

and sweets it's been turning out have become more fantastic and delicious all the time. And of course now when Mr Wonka invents some new and wonderful sweet, neither Mr Fickelgruber nor Mr Prodnose nor Mr Slugworth nor anybody else is able to copy it. No spies can go into the factory to find out how it is made.'

'But Grandpa, what sort of

people are they that work in there?'

'My dear boy,' said Grandpa Joe, 'that is one of the great mysteries of the chocolate-making world. We know only one thing about them. They are very small. The faint shadows that sometimes appear behind the windows, especially late at night when the lights are on, are those of *tiny* people, people no taller than my knee . . .'

'There aren't any such people,' Charlie said.

Just then, Mr Bucket,

Charlie's father, came into the room. He was home from the toothpaste factory, and he was waving an evening newspaper rather excitedly. 'Have you heard the news?' he cried. He held up the paper so that they could see the huge headline. The headline said:

WONKA FACTORY TO BE OPENED AT LAST TO LUCKY FEW

CHARLIE BUCKET and four
other **LUCKY** children have found
GOLDEN TICKETS inviting them
to visit **MR WILLY WONKA** at
his **CHOCOLATE FACTORY**.
THE BIG DAY HAS ARRIVED!

Greetings to you, the lucky finder of
this Golden Ticket, from Mr Willy
Wonka! I shake you warmly by the
hand! Many wonderful surprises await
you! For now, I do invite you to come
to my factory and be my guest for one

whole day — you and all others who are lucky enough to find my Golden Tickets. You must come to the factory gates at ten o'clock sharp in the morning. Don't be late! And you are allowed to bring with you either one or two members of your own family to ensure you don't get into mischief.

(signed) Willy Wonka

THE BIG DAY ARRIVES

Somewhere in the distance, a church clock began striking ten.

Very slowly, with a loud creaking of rusty hinges, the great iron gates of the factory began to swing open.

All eyes were fixed upon the gates.

'*There he is!*' somebody shouted.

'*That's him!*'

And so it was!

Mr Wonka was standing all alone just inside the open gates of the factory. And what an extraordinary little man he was!

He had a black top hat on his head.

He wore a tail coat made of a beautiful plum-coloured velvet.

His trousers were bottle green.

His gloves were pearly grey.

And in one hand he carried a fine gold-topped walking cane.

Covering his chin, there was a small, neat, pointed black beard – a goatee.

And his eyes – his eyes were most marvellously bright.

Colour me in!

They seemed to be sparkling and twinkling at you all the time. The whole face, in fact, was alight with fun and laughter.

And oh, how clever he looked! How quick and sharp and full of life!

He kept making quick jerky little movements with his head, cocking it this way and that, and taking everything in with those bright twinkling eyes. He was like a squirrel in the quickness of his movements, like a quick clever old squirrel from the park.

Suddenly, he did a funny little skipping dance in the snow, and he spread his arms wide, and he smiled at the five children who were clustered near the gates, and he called out, 'Welcome, my little friends! Welcome to the factory!' His voice was high and flutey. 'Will you come forward one at a time, please,' he called out, 'and bring your parents. Then show me your Golden Ticket and give me your name. Who's first?'

A big boy stepped up. 'I'm Augustus Gloop,' he said.

'Augustus!' cried Mr Wonka, seizing his hand and pumping it up and down with terrific force. 'My *dear* boy, how *good* to see you! Delighted! Charmed! Overjoyed to have you with us! And *these* are your parents? How *nice*! Come in! Come in! That's right! Step through the gates!'

Mr Wonka was clearly just as excited

as everybody else.

'My name,' said the next child to go forward, 'is Veruca Salt.'

'My *dear* Veruca! How *do* you do? What a pleasure this is! You *do* have an interesting name, don't you? I always thought that a veruca was a sort of wart that you got on the sole of your foot! But I must be wrong, mustn't I? How pretty you look in that lovely coat! I'm so glad you could come! Dear me, this is going to be *such* an exciting day! I *do* hope you enjoy it!

I'm sure you *will*! I *know* you will! Your father? How *are* you, Mr Salt? And Mrs Salt? Overjoyed to see you! Yes, the ticket is *quite* in order! Please go in!'

The next two children, Violet Beauregarde and Mike Teavee, came forward to have their tickets examined and then to have their arms practically pumped off their shoulders by the energetic Mr Wonka.

FACTORY FRIENDS

If you could take just one person with you to
the chocolate factory, who would you pick?
Draw a picture of the two of you
outside the gates.

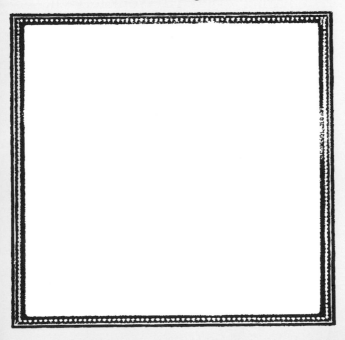

WELCOME TO THE CHOCOLATE FACTORY

Last of all, a small nervous voice whispered, 'Charlie Bucket.'

'Charlie!' cried Mr Wonka. 'Well, well, well! So *there* you are! You're the one who found your ticket only yesterday, aren't you? Yes, yes. I read *all* about it in this morning's papers! *Just* in time, my dear boy! I'm so glad! So happy for you! And this? Your grandfather?

Delighted to meet you, sir! Overjoyed! Enraptured! Enchanted! All right! Excellent! Is everybody in now? Five children? Yes! Good! Now will you please follow me! Our tour is about to begin! But *do* keep together! *Please* don't wander off by yourselves! I shouldn't like to lose any of you at *this* stage of the proceedings! Oh, dear me, no!'

Charlie glanced back over his shoulder and saw the great iron entrance gates slowly closing behind him. The crowds on the outside were pushing and shouting. Charlie took a last look at them. Then, as the gates closed with a clang, all sight of the outside world disappeared.

'Here we are!' cried Mr Wonka, trotting along in front of the group. 'Through this big red door, please! *That's* right! It's nice and warm inside!'

Charlie Bucket found himself standing in a long corridor that stretched away in front of him as far as he could see. The corridor was so wide that a car could easily have been driven along it. The walls were pale pink, the lighting was soft and pleasant.

'How lovely and warm!' whispered Charlie.

'I know. And what a marvellous smell!' answered Grandpa Joe, taking a long deep sniff. All the most wonderful smells in the world seemed to be mixed up in the air around them – the smell of roasting coffee and burnt sugar and melting chocolate and mint and violets and crushed hazelnuts and apple

43

blossom and caramel and lemon peel...

'Now *this*, my dear children,' said Mr
Wonka, raising his voice above the noise,
'this is the main corridor. Will you please
hang your coats and hats on those pegs
over there, and then follow me. *That's*
the way! Good! Everyone ready?
Come on, then! Here we go!'
He trotted off rapidly down the
corridor

with the tails of his plum-coloured velvet coat flapping behind him, and the visitors all hurried after him.

There were nine grown-ups and five children, fourteen in all. So you can imagine that there was a good deal of pushing and shoving as they hustled and bustled down the passage, trying to keep up with the swift little figure in front of them. 'Come *on*!' cried Mr Wonka. 'Get a move on, please! We'll *never* get round today if you dawdle like this!'

Soon, he turned right off the main

corridor into another slightly narrower passage.

Then he turned left.

Then left again.

Then right.

Then left.

Then right.

Then right.

Then left.

The place was like a gigantic rabbit warren, with passages leading this way and that in every direction.

'Don't you let go my hand, Charlie,'

whispered Grandpa Joe.

'Notice how all these passages are sloping downwards!' called out Mr Wonka. 'We are now going underground! *All* the most important rooms in my factory are deep down below the surface!'

Colour us in!

'Why is that?' somebody asked.

'There wouldn't be *nearly* enough space for them up on top!' answered Mr Wonka. 'These rooms we are going to see are *enormous*! They're larger than football fields! No building in the *world* would be big enough to house them!

But down here, underneath the ground, I've got *all* the space I want. There's no limit – so long as I hollow it out.'

Mr Wonka turned right.

He turned left.

He turned right again.

The passages were sloping steeper and steeper downhill now.

Then suddenly, Mr Wonka stopped. In front of him, there was a shiny metal door. The party crowded round. On the door, in large letters, it said:

THE CHOCOLATE ROOM

UNDERGROUND TUNNELS

Help Charlie find his way to the Chocolate Room through the twisty-turny tunnels of the factory.

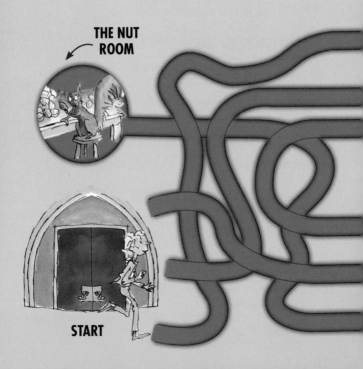

THE NUT ROOM

START

THE
CHOCOLATE
ROOM

THE
INVENTING
ROOM

Answer on page 62

THE CHOCOLATE ROOM

'An important room, this!' cried Mr
Wonka, taking a bunch of keys from
his pocket and slipping one into
the keyhole of the door. '*This* is
the nerve centre of the whole
factory, the
heart
of the
whole
business! And
so *beautiful*! I
insist upon my

rooms being beautiful! I can't *abide* ugliness in factories! *In* we go, then! But *do* be careful, my dear children! Don't lose your heads! Don't get over-excited! Keep very calm!'

Mr Wonka opened the door. Five children and nine grown-ups pushed their ways in – and *oh*, what an amazing sight it was that now met their eyes!

They were looking down upon a lovely valley. There were green meadows on either side of the valley, and along the bottom of it there

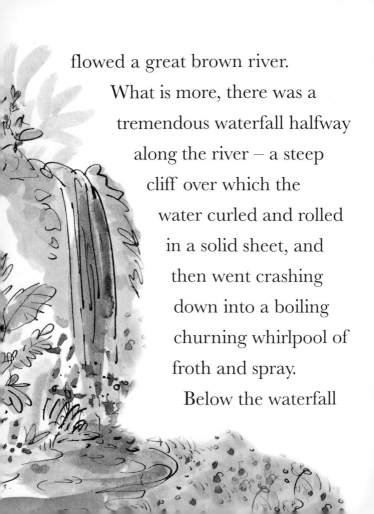

flowed a great brown river.
What is more, there was a
tremendous waterfall halfway
along the river – a steep
cliff over which the
water curled and rolled
in a solid sheet, and
then went crashing
down into a boiling
churning whirlpool of
froth and spray.
Below the waterfall

(and this was the most astonishing sight of all), a whole mass of enormous glass pipes were dangling down into the river from somewhere high up in the ceiling! They really were *enormous*, those pipes. There must have been a dozen of them at least, and they were sucking up the brownish muddy water from the river and carrying it away to goodness knows where. And because they were made of glass, you could see the liquid flowing and bubbling along inside them, and above the noise of the waterfall, you could hear the never-ending suck-suck-sucking sound of the pipes as they did their work.

Graceful trees and bushes were growing along the riverbanks – weeping willows and alders and tall clumps of rhododendrons with their pink and red and mauve blossoms. In the meadows there were thousands of buttercups.

'Do you like my trees?' Mr Wonka cried, pointing with his stick. 'And my lovely bushes? Don't you think they look pretty? Of course they are *all* eatable! All made of something different and delicious! And do you like my meadows? Do you like my grass and my buttercups? The grass you are standing on, my dear little ones, is made of a new kind of soft, minty sugar that I've just invented! I call it swudge! Try a blade!

Please do! It's delectable!'

The children and their parents were too flabbergasted to speak. They were staggered. They were dumbfounded. They were bewildered and dazzled.

They were completely bowled over by the hugeness of the whole thing. They simply stood and stared.

Find out more about WONDERFUL MR WILLY WONKA by visiting ROALDDAHL.COM

FANTASTICAL FACTORY

What sort of chocolate factory
would you build if you could?
List some of the
fantastical rooms here:

_____

_____

_____

_____

Use your stickers to decorate the inside of the factory!

ANSWERS

SEARCH AND FIND

Grandpa Joe's scarf is red.

PP.16–17. RUMOUR MILL

1. TRUE

2. FALSE – he has invented more than two hundred different types of chocolate bar!

3. FALSE – the eggs are blue with black spots.

4. TRUE

P.50–51. UNDERGROUND TUNNELS

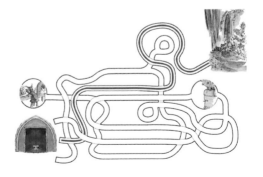

ROALD
DAHL